SATOMI ICHIKAWA

Bravo, Tanya

Story by

PATRICIA LEE GAUCH

PAPERSTAR

The Putnam & Grosset Group

Tiny Tanya loved to dance. She and her ballerina bear, Barbara, danced anywhere, anytime. Sometimes they did their *pas de deux* in the meadow. Sometimes by the brook. Sometimes to music only they heard.

Tanya loved to dance so much that her mother sent
her to dancing class with her sister, Elise. Barbara had to
stay in her bag.

At the first class Tanya was very happy. She put on her slippers and her leotard, just like all the dancers. When they went to the barre, she did, too. She walked just so, like a ballerina. And when Miss Bessinger said, "First position," Tanya already knew it. She knew second, fourth, and fifth, as well.

But when the woman with the comb in her hair began to play the piano, and Miss Bessinger clapped her hands and spoke at the same time, "One, two, three, four. One, two, three, four," Tanya could not hear any music at all.

Clap, clap, clap, clap. "One, two, three, four,"
is what she heard. And so when Miss Bessinger said,
"*Jeté*," Tanya was one jeté behind.

When Miss Bessinger said, "*Pirouette*," Tanya twirled
into the girl with a ponytail. And when Miss Bessinger
came up and whispered just to her, "ONE, TWO,

THREE, FOUR!'' when everyone was
doing an *arabesque*, Tanya teetered and fell. This didn't
feel like dancing at all.

Still each Saturday Tanya took Barbara
and went to class anyway.

By trying very hard, most of the time she kept in step
for the *glissades*. She finally did an arabesque and even
a *grand écart*.

Then one day when all of the parents came to visit and the dancers were all in a line doing *saut de chats*, the piano was so loud, Miss Bessinger's counting was so loud, Tanya stopped short and the other dancers danced right into her.

"It's all right," she heard Miss Bessinger tell her mother later. "Not everyone is a dancer. She is a lovely child, and she is enjoying herself, and that is what matters."

So Tanya took Barbara and started home ahead of her mother and Elise. She wasn't a lovely child, and she wasn't enjoying herself. Not at all.

Down by the brook she stopped. She just wanted to sit, but her ballerina bear, Barbara, didn't. Barbara wanted to dance.

"Well, all right," Tanya said. And so they did their pas
de deux on the rocks by the brook.

And next to the waterfall where the brook came from
the hill.

And near the woods where the branches sang.

Then Barbara was the audience while Tanya danced all alone in the meadow where she could hear the music in the wind.

Tanya didn't even see the piano player with the comb in her hair hiking across the field. And she didn't see her stop and watch with Barbara.

But when Tanya finally stopped dancing, she heard the clapping. It was a different kind from Miss Bessinger's. ''Bravo,'' the piano player said.

Tanya was so surprised her cheeks grew pink. "You like the music here," the piano player said. "I do, too." The sun made the lady's hair shine on top. "When I play the piano, sometimes I hear the wind. Sometimes I hear a storm. Sometimes I hear waves on a beach." Both Tanya and Barbara were surprised at that.

"Bravo, again," she said, and smiling, she got up and hiked across the field.

The next Saturday Tanya tucked Barbara into her bag and went to dance class.

When Miss Bessinger said, "Stretch," Tanya stretched.
When she said, first and second, fourth and fifth position,
plié and jeté, Tanya did. She even did more than one saut
de chat.

But when Miss Bessinger clapped—
one, two, three, four, one, two, three, four—
Tanya listened to the piano instead. She
heard waves, a storm, and branches in the
wind. And she danced.

"My goodness," Miss Bessinger said
later. "What a little ballerina you are!"

When she left that day, Tanya smiled at the piano player with the comb in her hair as she walked across the floor.

Every Saturday Tanya went to dance class. Her ballerina bear, Barbara, went, too. She went to the barre and she danced every step.

But Tanya and Barbara still liked best to dance a pas de deux, sometimes in the meadow, sometimes by the brook. Sometimes to music only they heard.

Printed on recycled paper

Library of Congress Cataloging-in-Publication Data
Gauch, Patricia Lee, Bravo, Tanya / by Patricia Lee Gauch; illustrated by Satomi Ichikawa.   p.   cm.
Summary: Tanya loves to dance but has trouble integrating her steps with the clapping and counting of her ballet teacher,
until she tries moving to the music and the sounds inside her head.   [1. Ballet dancing—Fiction.]   I. Ichikawa, Satomi, ill.
II. Title.   PZ7.G2315Br   1992   [E]—dc20   91-16005 CIP AC   ISBN 0-698-11391-8
3 5 7 9 10 8 6 4 2